The Grumpy Little Girls and the Princess Party

D1638525

Maisie

BESTEST FRIEND: Lulu

PETS: Only the Blob – (my baby brother!)

FAVOURITE GAME: Let's Pretend!

YUMMIEST FOOD: Slimy worms (Spaghetti, silly!)

SCARIEST SCARY THING: Spiders. Eeeek!

GETS GRUMPY: When Lulu won't play Let's Pretend...

FIZ

REAL NAME: Felicity. Yurgh!

BESTEST THING: Bouncing on my trampoline

WANTS V V V V MUCH: To learn to do a proper cartwheel

HATES: Playing quietly indoors

GETS GRUMPY: When my big brothers sit on me...

Ruby

favourite Cat

LOVES: Horse riding and karate lessons

HATES: Piano lessons. Snore!

WANTS V V V V MUCH: A pony and pierced ears. (But mum says I've got to wait till I'm 12!)

FAVOURITE COLOUR: Pink, pink, pink!

GETS GRUMPY: When Maisie and Lulu and Fiz won't do what I tell them...

LULU

BESTEST FRIEND: Maisie. (Or Warren, my woodlouse.)

PETS: 3 cats, 12 fish, 2 guinea pigs, 4 Giant Amazonian snails, 1 rabbit, 1 rat, 1 woodlouse

WANTS V V V MUCH: A ferret!

YUKKIEST FOOD: Meat

GETS GRUMPY: When mum makes me clean out my pets' cages...

First published in Great Britain by HarperCollins*Publishers* Ltd in 2000

1 3 5 7 9 10 8 6 4 2

ISBN: 0 00 664708 1

Concept copyright © Arroyo Projects 2000

Text and characters copyright © Lindsay Camp 2000

Illustrations copyright © Daniel Postgate 2000

The author and illustrator assert the moral right to be identified
as the author and illustrator of the work.

A CIP catalogue record for this title is available from the British Library. All rights reserved.
No part of this publication may be reproduced, stored in a retrieval system or transmitted
in any form or by any means, electronic, mechanical, photocopying, recording or otherwise,
without the prior permission of HarperCollins*Publishers* Ltd,
77-85 Fulham Palace Road, Hammersmith, London W6 8JB.

The HarperCollins website address is:
www.**fire**and**water**.com

Printed and bound in Singapore.

The Grumpy Little Girls and the Princess Party

Lindsay Camp and Daniel Postgate

Collins

An imprint of HarperCollinsPublishers

Her Supreme Loveliness Princess Zelda Imelda-Mae
was feeling grumpy.

It was almost her birthday and she'd commanded her
Chief Lady-in-Waiting to organise a Princess Party.

"Oh Maisie," said her mum, "wouldn't you rather do something else?"

"No," said Princess Zelda Imelda-Mae. "And don't call me Maisie, or I'll have you thrown into my deepest, darkest dungeon."

"I know what," said her mum. "We could take Lulu, Ruby and Fiz to see a film, and go for a pizza afterwards."

"Princesses hate pizza," said Princess Zelda Imelda-Mae. "I want a Princess Party, and that's that."

"Hmm," said her mum. "I'll have to ask the King what he thinks about it."

Next day, before school, Maisie handed out the invitations.

Lulu and Ruby were very excited, but Fiz was a bit grumpy.

"I hate dressing up," she panted, skipping hard.

"It's OK," said Maisie, who was in a good mood. "I don't mind if you come in your dungarees."

"As long as you wear a crown," said Ruby, firmly.

By order of
Her Supreme Loveliness
Princess Zelda Imelda-Mae,
you are commanded to attend
a Princess Party.

On the day of the party, Maisie woke up very early indeed. She put on her long sparkly princess dress straight away.

"Is it nearly half past three?" she asked, for the fifth time, just after breakfast.

"Not quite yet, Your Fabulous Gorgeousness," replied her dad.

"Oh, I can't wait for my Princess Party," sighed Maisie.

At last the doorbell rang, and there was Lulu – who arrived first because she only lived next door. Maisie gasped. She'd never seen Lulu looking so... princess-ish.

"Greetings, Princess Zelda Imelda-Mae," said Princess Lulu, handing over her present.

And after that, the doorbell kept ringing, and more and more princesses arrived, all looking very beautiful – even Princess Fiz, who was wearing a shiny silver tutu over her dungarees.

But for some reason, Maisie found she wasn't really enjoying herself. There was something not quite right about this Princess Party...

"Let's start the games,"said Maisie's dad.

"But Ruby isn't here yet,"said Lulu.

Just then, the doorbell rang once more, and into the room swept Princess Ruby.

Everybody stopped what they were doing and stared. Ruby's mum made costumes for TV programmes, and the princess dress she'd made for Ruby was absolutely brilliant.

It was all shimmery, and there were millions of jewels – rubies, of course – sewn all over it. A long floaty bit trailed along the ground.

Ruby did a twirl, and everyone started to clap!

Everyone except Maisie – who ran out of the room and up the stairs, screaming, "It's not fair! It's my party and I want to be the most beautiful princess!"

"Oh dear," said Maisie's dad, following her.

"Who wants to play Musical Thrones?" asked Maisie's mum.

Upstairs, Maisie slammed her
bedroom door behind her.
Her dad knocked gently.

"Excuse me, Your Utter Beautifulness, your loyal subjects are awaiting your majestic presence downstairs."

"Go away, not playing, stupid game!" shouted Maisie.

"All right, Maisie," said her dad. "You can come down when you've stopped being so silly."

Maisie knew she had been silly, very silly to have a Princess Party. She should have had a Servants and Slaves Party, and then she would have been the only princess.

She lay on her bed, listening to the others shouting and laughing downstairs and feeling very grumpy indeed... until suddenly, she heard a scream.

It sounded like Lulu.

aisie crept to the top of the stairs to see what was the matter.
It **was** Lulu, holding something small in her hand, and howling.

"What happened?" asked Maisie, coming downstairs.

"Fiz killed Warren!" wailed Lulu.

Fiz was looking miserable, too. And she'd gone bright red.

"It was an accident," explained Maisie's mum. "Fiz was bouncing
on the sofa, and she landed on the matchbox
with Lulu's pet woodlouse in it."

"He's completely squashed!" sobbed Lulu.

"Poor Warren," said Maisie, forgetting
her own grumpiness.

And then she had a good idea.
"Come upstairs with me, everyone,"
she said. "We need to get changed."

"This isn't a Princess Party any more," explained Maisie. "It's a Burying Warren Party. We're going to bury him in the garden."

And so they did.

With Lulu behind her, carrying the squashed matchbox, Maisie led everyone out into the garden.

"What do we do now?" said Ruby, who was rather grumpy about having to take off her beautiful princess dress.

"Shhh!" said Maisie. "I'm going to say a poem..."

"O Warren," she began, "you were wonderful,

And you belonged to Lulu.

But now that you've been squashed by Fiz,

I'm sure we're going to miss you."

Then they all sang a sad song that they had learned at school about an old donkey, because they didn't know any songs about woodlice.

Very carefully, Fiz dug a little hole and Lulu put the matchbox into it, and covered it with soil.

"We need a stone to put on top," said Maisie. "So we'll remember where he is."

"What about this one?" said Fiz, picking up a huge rock.

"Oh look!" said Ruby, pointing.

Under where the rock had been, was the most enormous woodlouse.

Lulu's eyes lit up. "Oh, please can I have him? Please, please, please!"

"Of course you can," said Maisie's mum. "I'll find a matchbox for him."

"You can put him in your party bag," suggested Maisie, wondering why...

...she hadn't thought of
a Burying Warren Party
in the first place.

Maisie

BESTEST FRIEND: Lulu

PETS: Only the Blob – (my baby brother!)

FAVOURITE GAME: Let's Pretend!

YUMMIEST FOOD: Slimy worms (Spaghetti, silly!)

SCARIEST SCARY THING: Spiders. Eeeek!

GETS GRUMPY: When Lulu won't play Let's Pretend...

FIZ

REAL NAME: Felicity. Yurgh!

BESTEST THING: Bouncing on my trampoline

WANTS V V V V MUCH: To learn to do a proper cartwheel

HATES: Playing quietly indoors

GETS GRUMPY: When my big brothers sit on me...

Ruby

LOVES: Horse riding and karate lessons

HATES: Piano lessons. Snore!

WANTS V V V V MUCH: A pony and pierced ears. (But mum says I've got to wait till I'm 12!)

FAVOURITE COLOUR: Pink, pink, pink!

GETS GRUMPY: When Maisie and Lulu and Fiz won't do what I tell them...

LULU

favourite Cat

BESTEST FRIEND: Maisie. (Or Warren, my woodlouse.)

PETS: 3 cats, 12 fish, 2 guinea pigs, 4 Giant Amazonian snails, 1 rabbit, 1 rat, 1 woodlouse

WANTS V V V MUCH: A ferret!

YUKKIEST FOOD: Meat

GETS GRUMPY: When mum makes me clean out my pets' cages...

Have you read all the stories about us?

The Grumpy Little Girls and the Princess Party
ISBN 0 00 664708 1

The Grumpy Little Girls and the Wobbly Sleepover
ISBN 0 00 664709 X

The Grumpy Little Girls and the Bouncy Ferret
ISBN 0 00 664770 7

The Grumpy Little Girls and the Naughty Little Boy
ISBN 0 00 664769 3